THE DAY I MET THE
Sock Monster

••••••••••• TRISH WEYMOUTH •••••••••••

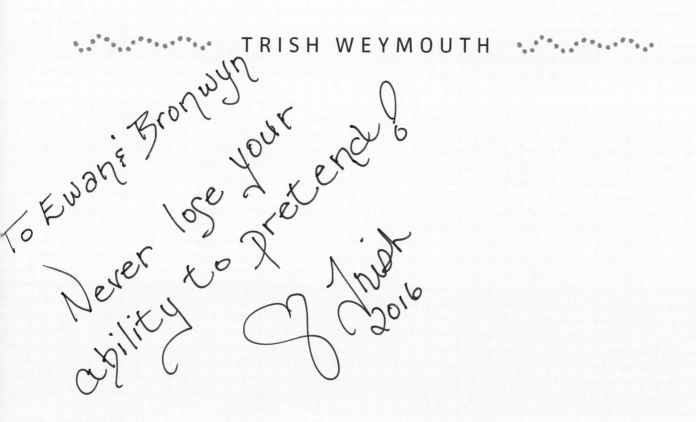

To Ewan & Bronwyn
Never lose your
ability to Pretend!
♡ Trish
2016

Tellwell Talent
www.tellwell.ca

ISBN
Paperback: 978-1-987985-72-6
Hardcover: 978-1-987985-71-9

When I was very young, I remember Mom complaining about all the laundry she had to do. Who could blame her, there were three of us kids plus Dad and Mom all living at home, and we would change our clothes a lot during the day!

We wore our newer clean clothes to school. After school we changed into our play clothes. We also played sports, so we had our uniforms, socks, and gear that needed to be washed too. To top it off Mom and Dad had all their clothes that needed washing as well.

I didn't understand why doing laundry was such a big deal....it looked like fun to me!

I found out soon enough that doing laundry was the least of Mom's worries, for every time she did laundry I would find her scratching her head and saying to herself: *"I am sure we have a sock monster in our laundry room."*

A sock monster?! I could not believe my ears!! I was always told there was no such thing as monsters. I guess Mom and Dad only told us that so we would not worry, but I had heard it with my own ears...there really was a sock monster!

Every time Mom would send me down to the basement to get her something she needed from the laundry room, my heart would beat so fast I thought it would JUMP right out of my throat!

My palms would get sweaty and my knees would turn to rubber. I would call my trusty dog to help me with my assignment and arm myself with a broom. Then slowly, ever so carefully, I would descend into the dreaded basement.

As soon as I gathered what Mom needed, we would turn around as fast as we could and bolt back up the steps. I climbed up three stairs at a time! When I reached the top I was completely out of breath and proud, knowing that once again I had outsmarted the ever elusive...

SOCK MONSTER!!

One rainy day I was interrupted from watching television in the living room for my next big assignment. Mom wanted me to go down to the laundry room and find her special tablecloth because we were having company over for dinner. Once again my heart began beating faster, my palms got sweaty, and my knees turned to jelly. In fact my knees began to knock together so hard I was getting bruises!

I called my trusty dog to come with me, but when he didn't come I suddenly remembered he was at the groomers getting a bath and a haircut.

NO DOG!!!

Now what was I going to do? I had never before braved the basement by myself. I tried to stall for time, but Mom would not buy it. Our company would be arriving soon, so she needed the table-cloth now!

I went to the broom closet and grabbed my dependable broom. Once again I slowly descended the steps to the basement. It seemed like days had passed before I finally reached the laundry room. My mouth was so dry that it felt like I had cotton balls in it. I inched toward the shelves by the dryer. I began looking through the boxes on the shelf, checking behind me every few seconds or so.

Then **Crash!!!**

I turned quickly and grabbed my broom. Terrified at what I might find, I looked between the shelves and the dryer. There, huddled in a little ball, peeking through his fingers... WAS THE SOCK MONSTER!!!

I couldn't believe my eyes! I wanted to scream, but the scream got stuck in my throat. I looked at the strange little creature. He was all furry. He had big green eyes with very long eyelashes, he also had one leg with a large foot at the end of it, and two long hairy arms. He uncovered his eyes, and then carefully balanced himself on his arms. Then I heard a teeny, squeaky little voice say "P-p-p-pleeeease don't hurt me. I didn't mean to scare you." I didn't know what to say. He looked so tiny and sad.

W hat are you doing down here?" I finally managed to ask. "Well," he began, "I never meant to hurt anyone, but my foot gets so cold at night that I need a sock to keep it warm. I come from very large family and we all need socks. So when no one is around I come and take some of your socks." I thought for a moment, and then I said, "That's stealing! Don't you know that?"

"Well, I do know that," he said, "but we have no other way to get the socks, and we need to keep our feet warm or we will get very sick. I tried getting a job as a sales person at a clothing store, but the manager freaked out when she saw I was not an actual "PERSON" but a "MONSTER". Then I tried to get a job at a fast food place, but the manager said not only was I a monster, but I was so hairy the customers would definitely complain about hair in there lunch. I tried many more places but it was the same sad story everywhere I went. I thought it would be so simple, all I wanted was to buy socks, but no matter what I did or said the answer was always "Sorry, we do not hire Monsters! So in the end I found it much easier to just take your socks."

I looked long and hard at the Sock Monster's sad little face. He had huge tears welling up in his eyes.

"You're not going to tell on me, are you?" he whimpered. How could I resist his sweetness? I was stuck. What was I going to do about this mess? I finally came up with a great idea.

Okay," I said, "here's the plan. You can borrow the socks, but somewhere along the way you are going to have to return them. You can put them back in places where people won't expect them, so they will just think that they were misplaced."

The little Sock Monster ran over and jumped into my arms. "I don't know how I will ever repay you for your kindness!" he said, with tears running down his cheeks.

"Well," I said, "You could be my FRIEND!" So the deal was made. The Sock Monster and I became great friends.

But as all little kids do, I grew up. Over the years I saw less and less of my little friend, until one day he was gone forever...or so I thought!

Now that I'm a mom with kids of my own, my family goes through a mountain of laundry every week. Every laundry day, I find myself repeating those oh so famous words of my mother:

"I AM SURE WE MUST HAVE A SOCK MONSTER IN OUR LAUNDRY ROOM!"

The End

or is it?......

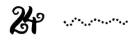